The *Beatrix Potter* Gardener's Year Book

With an introduction for each month by

Caroline Kennedy

SOURCES

The Beatrix Potter paintings used in this year book are reproduced
by courtesy of the following:

The Armitt Trust: October, picture 1 and pine cone border;
November, picture 2 and fungus border

The Trustees of the Linder Collection, Book Trust: January, picture 1;
February, picture 1; May, picture 2 and foxglove border; July, picture 2;
August, carnation border; September, apple border; October, acorn border;
November, picture 1 and leaves border; December, leaves border

Sotheby's: July, picture 1

Frederick Warne Archive: March, picture 1; April, picture 1;
December, picture 1

The remaining pictures are reproduced by courtesy of
The National Art Library, Victoria and Albert Museum

FREDERICK WARNE

Published by the Penguin Group
27 Wrights Lane, London W8 5TZ, England
Penguin Books USA Inc., 375 Hudson Street, New York, New York 10014, USA
Penguin Books Australia Ltd, Ringwood, Victoria, Australia
Penguin Books Canada Ltd, 10 Alcorn Avenue, Toronto, Ontario, Canada MV4 3B2
Penguin Books (NZ) Ltd, 182-190 Wairau Road, Auckland 10, New Zealand

First published 1991
1 3 5 7 9 10 8 6 4 2

Text copyright © Caroline Kennedy, 1991

ISBN 0 7232 3714 X

Colour origination by Anglia Graphics Ltd.
Printed and bound in Great Britain by
William Clowes Limited, Beccles and London

ABOUT THE AUTHOR

Caroline Kennedy studied garden design and horticulture
as a second career and now runs her own business designing
gardens and overseeing their planting and development. She
travels extensively and has studied garden styles in America, Europe,
Australasia and North Africa. She divides her time between London
and Norfolk, lecturing regularly on garden design and methods.
She lives in the country in Norfolk, where, in the last five years, she
has created the kind of garden Beatrix Potter would approve
of - a charming country garden with an orchard, a cottage
garden, greenhouse, formal areas, and a woodland
garden out of two acres of mainly jungle!
This is her first book.

January

Snow in Beatrix Potter's garden in the Lake District,
11 January 1913

*My grandmother says that when it snows in
Hertfordshire it lies all winter. . . At such times of frost and snow the two
great cedars in the lawn look their best.   The snow lies in wreaths on
their broad outstretched arms, or, melting, trickles down the
dusty green bark with red stains.*

Memories of Camfield Place, Journal c. 1881

After Christmas comes deep winter, the dormant season for growing. If the weather is calm and frozen, the beauty of the countryside is etched, almost in monochrome. Grasses and reeds are reflected in frozen water, their stalks and seedheads encrusted with frost. Trees and shrubs become charcoal silhouettes.

January is the coldest month of the year and brings a series of meteorological hazards to be survived. Heavy cloud and long periods of rain may precede some of the coldest nights of the year and this combination can cause frost damage to soft brickwork and porous pots which absorb water and are then cracked by ice. All the gardener can do is to try to minimise the effects of adverse weather. Plants will often survive well under a complete cover of snow, but if they protrude above the snow can become badly frosted. On the other hand, heavy snow should be knocked off evergreen hedges and branches to prevent damage. Having done all he can, the stoic gardener may find time best spent browsing through catalogues of seeds and herbaceous plants for the spring, knowing that all gardeners work with an ever-receding ideal of perfection.

During intervals of relatively calm weather it is worth venturing out to inspect the damage. Picking one's way across the sodden ground and avoiding the constant dripping, one may well reflect that the charms of a winter garden cannot compete with a good fire but it does offer its own quiet pleasures.

This is the time when tiny pale blooms of bare stemmed shrubs are most cherished and appreciated. Winter flowering jasmine with green stems and clusters of pale yellow flowers is very obliging and will thrive in almost any position, even on a cold sunless north wall. It will also perform in all sorts of awkward corners as a twiggy sprawl with its long summer growths now transformed into a mass of fresh yellow. Winter sweet, a deliciously scented shrub adorned with pale waxy flowers, yellow outer petals and shorter purple inner ones, like tufts of waxy spikes, grows happily as a free standing shrub allowed to make its own shape. If you train it against a wall, it will require pruning after flowering which seems to prevent flowering for another two years. The third member of this trio is witch hazel. A shrub of great character with its slow twisted growth and flowers made of a fringe of crinkled gold, it is very hardy and stands up to cold winds. If you cut twigs to bring indoors, the blooms are long lasting and decorative, filling a whole room with their fragrance. Chinese witch hazel reveals its true Asiatic character on a frosty morning, its oriental silhouette encrusted with frost and its yellow tassels candied with white crystals.

The most vivacious feature in the garden at this time of year is probably the bird table and any shallow unfrozen pond or birdbath. Flocks of starlings arrive for bathing parties to keep their feathers clean and fluffy which greatly enhances the insulating qualities of plumage through those long frozen winter nights. Flocks of finches will feed on flowerheads left to run to seed. If you decide to provision a bird table, this is a responsibility which must be taken seriously all winter as you will soon develop a throng of hungry dependants who will starve if you stop.

If you feed after breakfast just as it gets light birds can emerge from a freezing night for vital food. House sparrows, tits and finches have tough beaks and can crack sunflower seeds and corn. Coaltits are fond of peanuts. But insect eaters need soft food like lumps of fat or cheese. Beware of the cat - put the bird table at least two yards from the nearest cover-providing shrub and make it at least five foot high or even hanging from a tree. Many birds like to land on a branch to investigate before feeding, or need a handy retreat if there is danger. Most important of all, from the provider's point of view, the feeding station should be within good viewing from your busiest windows so that you can enjoy the drama all day.

January

Birds feeding in a walled garden at Tenby, Pembrokeshire

January

January

A snow scene looking across a tarn
to a wooded hillside

February

A bowl of snowdrops

My garden is a case of the survival of the fitest [sic] - *always*
very full of flowers and weeds, presently it will be a sheet of self-sown
snowdrops, and later on daffodils.

Letter to Caroline Clark, 1930

February is a dark, damp month but the gardener knows that there is frenetic activity under the ground. The cold and frost can be interrupted by false springs of warm weather which encourage early growth. Soft green growth will inevitably be scorched by the frost unless it can be protected. This is the month for making the most use of glass: the greenhouse, the cold frame and cloches. Otherwise we can enjoy a clear conscience about garden chores.

Amidst all this gloom the two true messengers of spring appear: first the aconite with buttercup yellow bravado, and then the delicate demure 'Fair Maid of February', the snowdrop. It seems miraculous that the nose of such a small bulb has the strength to push through the ice-hard earth. The snowdrop is the image of delicacy with its fresh white pendant flowers trimmed with pure green markings. Both aconites and snowdrops look wonderful in the wild, carpeting the woodland floor, but this effect can be copied by planting as many as possible around the winter skeletons of deciduous shrubs, so that they can enjoy semi shade when the summer comes, and a cool moist situation. They make a particularly fine picture in February massed round native hazel, or even corkscrew hazel, with a display of fine catkins, looking almost grey in dull weather but golden in winter sunshine.

It is a myth that the winter garden is sombre. When there are few other distractions the beauty of bark and stem can be appreciated. All winter the silver and charcoal patterns on birch trunks have been gleaming, especially when the trees have been planted as a clump, or three in one hole, to give the impression of a multi-stemmed tree. Native holly and yew work well as a dark contrasting background to silver birches and other multi-stemmed shrubs like willows and dogwoods.

Willows create the right atmosphere for an informal boundary to the garden, the stumpy trunks anchoring the display of fantastic doodling shapes created by the topknot of stems. Even when snow covers the ground a warm sparkle of colour emanates from the stems of the dogwood, fresher and brighter if they are cut back annually in the spring. Between the willows and the dogwoods there is a surprisingly wide range of colour display: purple black stems on *Salix melanostachys*; powdery white on *Salix nigricans*; *Salix caprea* has silvery grey buds accompanied by catkins tinged with pink; scarlet stems shoot from *Salix Britensis* and yellow from *Salix vitellina*; sealing wax red is contributed by *Cornus Westonbirt* and yellow by *Cornus flaviramea*. The last four are best planted as a thicket of only one variety so that their effect is enhanced by numbers.

February is the month for comparing and contrasting the merits of different hellebores. In a semi-wild corner perhaps the stinking hellebore, which has been flowering since December, would be chosen for its large green flowers and evergreen deeply divided dark green leaves. In a shaded corner in more formal parts of the garden the Corsican hellebore might be preferred with its delicate apple green flowers gathered in large heads amongst more symmetrical leathery leaves. The Lenten rose is evergreen with less distinguished leaves but flowers in a range of colours including cream, an almost bruised purple, and creamy pink. It mixes well with the plum purple and green flowers of *Helleborus atrorubens*. To complement these creamy and greeny flowers it is hard to think of a better companion than *Arum italicum* 'Pictum', its dark green fresh leaves veined with creamy white. The Christmas rose makes up the collection of hellebores with its spectacular waxy white flowers carried in thicker posies nearer to the ground. It does not flower in time for Christmas unless given the extra protection of a cloche.

The garden in February introduces us to a subtle, sophisticated palette of colours which is unique to this month: green and white, dark reds, purpley blacks, greeny yellows and golden yellows. All of these mix well together in informal planting schemes and are sometimes graced by a surprise visit from an early primrose with its clear pale yellow petals and crinkly matt green leaves, making a promise of spring in a few sheltered inches of the garden.

February

A garden scene with water butt, basket and, in the
background, a cold frame.

February

February

GARDEN DESIGN

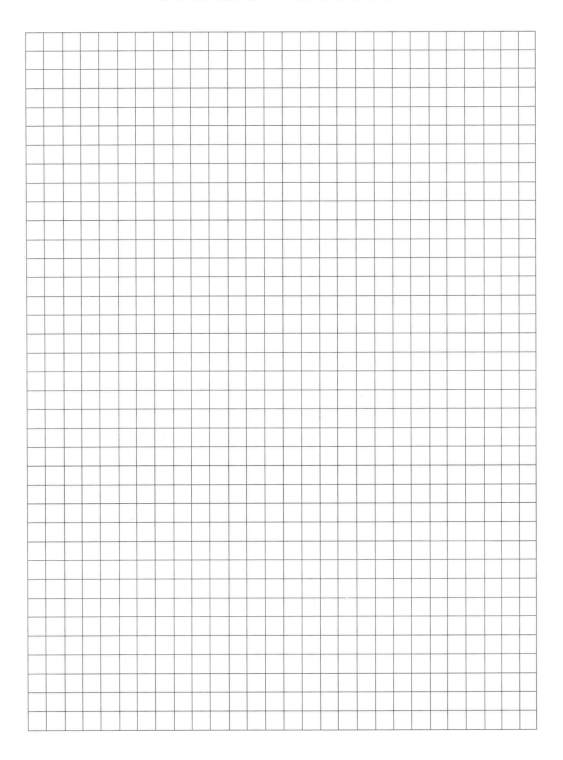

March

Mr. Pricklepin from *Appley Dapply's Nursery Rhymes*

At present it is nice weather for gardening. Some plants have perished, through damp and through a sharp frost upon rain ... The garden is not seriously weedy. It is carpetted [sic] with jonquils and spring flowers.

Letter to Caroline Clark, March 18 1939

The mad March hare is an appropriate symbol for this month of tantalising contrasts: on the one hand, a change in the season is boldly advertised by the strong, rich yellows of forsythia and daffodils so we are enticed into a mood of anticipation; while, on the other, late frosts and cold drying winds wreak havoc with soft, new leaf growth and buds on flowering shrubs. March is the month of the greatest daily variation in the weather: warm afternoon sunshine can seduce gardeners into thinking that spring has arrived and embarking on sowing and planting which may be caught by a vicious cold spell.

Another spring hazard is the activity of slugs who revel in the feasts provided by young seedlings in wet weather and the succulent young leaves of hostas beginning to push up. Toads and hedgehogs in their turn prey on slugs but do not seem to keep up. The gardener who wants to work with nature is faced with a dilemma. If slug pellets are put down they may be consumed, inside the slugs, by birds, toads and hedgehogs and, therefore, be fatal to friends as well as foes. Two ecologically acceptable solutions are to put down half grapefruits, inverted, or beakers of beer, sunk into the ground, to attract slugs, which can then be escorted off the premises.

On a fine day in March there is plenty to discover and reward wrapping up and venturing out. The japanese quince, *Japonica*, with saucer shaped flowers varying from crimson to pale pink with golden anthers, glows from a sheltered wall. *Magnolia stellata*'s star-shaped flowers with fresh, white strap-like petals, emerge from hairy, grey winter buds. Flowering currants can be picked and brought into the house to open a paler shade of pink. Scent wafts from bunches of creamy white, waxy flowers of the winter honeysuckle. The strongest scent comes from a surprising source - the neat, mounded evergreen *Daphne odora aureo-marginata*, its apple green leaves rimmed with cream to set off magenta pink buds, opening to off-white flowers.

Besides enjoying a treasure hunt in the garden, serious work begins in March. Clumps of snowdrops can be split up now and made into new plantings 'in the green'. Snowdrops are best left undisturbed for at least four years but, after that, when the tips of the leaves are turning yellow, use a fork to lift a crowded clump out of the ground. Separate the bulbs and re-plant as soon as possible at the same depth as they were previously. Now is the time to get the mower's blades oiled and sharpened and to prune the roses. If the weather is frost-free, you can begin early in March.

This is display time for the soft colours of small spring bulbs planted around the skirts of deciduous shrubs. Naturalised crocuses make clumps of mauve, yellow and white, drifting into the lawn. Glory-of-the-snow has the intense blue of a mountain sky. Star-shaped flowers with white centres appear before the leaves and its flowering is soon followed by its close relative, the Spanish squill, or *Scilla*, with brilliant blue, nodding, bell-shaped flowers. The daisy like flowers of the windflower make luminous carpets of pale blue, pink and white, especially effective in the half shade on the north side of the house.

Little daffodils planted in a special position near the house, reward that care now. The dainty hoop petticoat daffodil, *Narcissus bulbocodium*, only four to six inches tall, is exquisite. The more robust varieties of *Narcissus cyclamineus*, sporting upward-sweeping petals and cheerful names, like 'Peeping Tom', 'Tete à tete' and 'Jack Snipe' mill about in bright groups along the front of the border, brightening up awkward corners before perennials begin to shoot.

A particular pleasure of anticipation in March is the sight of plum red paeony shoots pushing up through the bare soil and the fresh green shoots of day lilies. There is an excitement and expectancy in the air and these are pledges of the garden re-awakening.

Sewing Seeds - Broad Beans, Broccoli, Brussels Sprouts, Winter Cabbage, Garlic, Leek, Onion, Early Crop Peas, Perpetual Summer Spinach,

---

Artichokes - Beginning of March

Peas (Kelvedon Wonder) 19th 26th 1st Row.

Cabbage (Golden Acre) 26th One Row

Broccoli - Summer Purple Sprouting 26th One Row

Brussels Sprouts   26th One Row.

Gardening in Tenby, Pembrokeshire

March

March

Polyanthus primroses

April

Bird's-eye view from Hill Top Farm, in *The Tale of Samuel Whiskers*

April is the month that real spring arrives: primroses in the woods, blossom on the trees and lambs in the fields make it feel like a sparkling fresh start. The sky is full of returning migrants, filling the garden with birdsong, as they dart, swoop and busy themselves building nests. Although the weather is often dreadful, when the sun does shine, it is surprisingly warm and, suddenly, it is good to be outside again.

Nature's colour scheme for April is white, fresh green of new grass, pale green of new leaves, clear primrose yellow and some strong blues, like grape hyacinth and early bluebells. These colours look very good transposed into the garden setting, if you choose white blossoming trees and shrubs, rather than the rich pinks and reds of imported cherries, which tend to clash with yellow and spring green and only look good against a dark evergreen background.

White blossom in spring is particularly vivid and fresh contrasted with bare branches. The first tree in the garden to produce a froth of white blossom is the snowy mespilus, its stark white flowers accompanied by the unfurling of soft, downy, bronze foliage. This slender tree can be grown as a multi-stemmed shrub and looks best when several are grouped together. Twiggy spiraea, or Bridal wreath, displays its pure white flower clusters, fresh as a dusting of snowflakes.

White narcissi look beautiful, especially *Narcissus triandrus* 'Thalia', with back-swept creamy petals, and *Narcissus poeticus* 'Actaea', or Pheasant's Eye, with a red-rimmed cup, smells heavenly and looks particularly fine planted informally in colonies in uncut grass or with wood spurge in a shady orchard. Narcissi should be planted in front of daffodils so that the dying leaves of the daffodils, which must be left to replenish the bulbs, fade into the background.

A mysterious and enigmatic companion for the extrovert narcissi is the snakeshead fritillary. It is easy to imagine that each scalloped bell-shaped flower has been hand-painted with its unique variation on the chequerboard design: whiteish green, pinkish lilac, reddish purple and bitter chocolate. The other miracle of April is lily-of-the-valley, thriving in dark corners, apparently as happy tucked in a narrow bed beneath a wall in a town garden as massed on a cool, shady woodland floor. The exquisitely scented flowers, set so decoratively against the stem, earned it the name of ladder-to-heaven in medieval times.

This is the real beginning of the gardening year: there is much to do and little time to do it and so wet weekends can be very frustrating. Memories of winter fade as the long daylight hours and frequent showers encourage new growth, not all of it welcome, as weeds also come to life with a vengeance. As soon as the frosts relent, cut the straggling middle-aged shoots of shrubby herbs, like artemesia, santolina, rue, russian sage and lavender, hard back to keep the plants shapely and foliage fresh and bright.

While attacking the spring crop of weeds, the gardener may well contemplate the benefits of ground cover, both practical and aesthetic. In the wild there is no bare earth but a thick cover of vegetation conserves moisture and most plants seem to do better growing close together. The planting formation of self-seeding wild plants, like primroses, can be copied in the garden and plants with beautiful leaves used to obtain attractive textural harmonies and contrasts. In April, many plants which are grown for their pleasing leaves are also flowering: bergenia has spoon shaped evergreen leaves and flowers varying from magenta to white; lungwort flowers vivid blue, pink and clear white with many variations of silver blotches and spots on matt green leaves; the foam flower's evergreen pale maple-like leaves will soon be decorated with creamy flower spikes. The new leaves of meadow crane's bills are making their own impact with domes of dark green, deeply lobed palmate leaves and the vigorous new shoots of hostas are full of promise.

April

SOW BEETROOT. (DETROIT 2 CRIMSON GLOBE) 3rd. ONE ROW

SPRING ONION (WHITE LISBON) 3rd ONE ROW

LETTUCE (LOBJOITS GREEN COS) 3rd ONE ROW.

Pheasant's Eye Narcissus

April

April

Photographs

May

Cowslips and bluebells

The woods are lovely now, wild cherry trees covered
with blossom as white as snow, and violets and primroses and
bluebells amongst the nut bushes.

Letter to June Steel, 8 May 1933

May is the loveliest month for woodland gardens. On acidic soil magnolias, azaleas and rhododendrons are coming into their prime, while chalky soil sustains a quieter display of Mexican orange blossom, tree paeonies and viburnums. In the wild, the skirted branches of beech trees support a luminous leaf canopy over carpets of bluebells and wood anemones. Sunlight filters through fresh foliage and creates pools of light and dappled shade where pale flowers catch the light and glisten like stars. Natural colours in May are pale creams, lemons, ivory, white and pale green. The occasional mass of colour, such as bluebells, is diffused by indirect light and so the whole effect is softened and fresh.

In the brief interval between the procession of bulbs and the development of full leaf cover there is a season for shade tolerant perennials. In a small garden a woodland glade can be created in the shade of one tree. To make the most of the dappled shade effect it is important to choose pale flowers and silver variegation or leaves. The arching stems of Solomon's Seal carry bell-shaped greeny white flowers which are particularly effective in a dark corner. Columbines are charming in plain white but tend to seed themselves and come up in all sorts of variations on the blue-mauve spectrum. The same might be said of the biennual foxglove which is very elegant in white, and proliferates in a crushed strawberry colour, *Digitalis mertonensis*, as well as the orthodox purple. The white form of bleeding heart, which bears its locket shaped flowers in arching sprays, seems to last longer than the pink and its fern like foliage remains surprisingly fresh for months. Variegated grasses, such as *Holcus mollis* 'Albo-variegatus' or the yellowy-green bracts of wood spurge lighten and complement this kind of planting and contrast beautifully with the blue spikes and bronzey leaves of bugle and purple or white honesty. The silvery carpeter, *Lamium maculatum*, 'Beacon Silver', is a useful illuminator. Hostas and shuttlecock ferns can be added if your soil is sufficiently moist. In a cherished part of the garden you might complete the picture with dog's tooth violets.

Despite these invitations to enchantment, May is a very busy time for gardeners. In periods of sunny dry weather the garden makes up for any checks that may have occurred in a cold spring. May is a stabilising month when plants respond rapidly to milder conditions. Everything is growing fast, especially weeds. Both the vegetable patch and herbaceous plants need to be hoed before the weeds take over. The soil should be left cultivated to a fine tilth to absorb rain and conserve water. It may already be necessary to begin watering and apply mulches to retain moisture.

Now clematis roots need to be kept cool by placing a stone or compost on the soil surface. Traditionally, there are supposed to be no more frosts after mid May, which means tender plants which have been grown in frames or the greenhouse can be planted outside after being 'hardened off'.

Fruit trees need some attention in May. If the fruit set appears good on apples, pears, plums and sweet cherries, they should be fed with sulphate of ammonia. If there is a food and moisture shortage now it will reduce the size of the fruit. The crop on young trees should be limited by rubbing out flower clusters or removing and thinning fruitlets by hand, leaving the leaf clusters to build up the tree.

Vigilance with roses is also necessary. Greenfly may be feasting on the succulent new growth and should be sprayed. If the leaves of roses have rolled up because of the presence of either a small green caterpillar of the tortrix moth or a small grey green grub of the sawfly, they should be removed and burned.

Gravel paths make an interesting study at this time because they sprout all sorts of seedlings as well as weeds. Rock plants, creeping jenny, lady's mantle, lavender, columbines, violas, bugle, and golden marjoram all thrive and self-seed on gravel which provides sharp drainage, thus reproducing the conditions of plant life in the mountains.

May

The Nuttery at Harescombe Grange, Gloucestershire,
Spring 1903

May

May

A garden scene, Gwaynynog, Denbigh

June

A posy of wild flowers including buttercup, cornflower,
forget-me-not, honeysuckle and scabious

The bees hum round the flowers, the air is laden with the smell
of roses ... and the deep low of the cattle comes answering one another
across the valley, borne on the summer breeze which sweeps
down through the woods from the heather moors.

Journal, 14 June 1884

The month of June is a treat for the sense of colour and the sense of smell: there is excitement as perennials break into flower, and colours, like the azure blue of delphiniums, bring the sparkling summer sky into the garden. The scents of roses and mock orange celebrate the arrival of summer.

During June the crop of wild flowers, mostly annuals and biennuals, proliferates on the verges of country roads and round ripening wheatfields. Oxeye daisies, poppies, sweet rocket, clovers, pink campion and cornflowers carpet these starved strips of land and inspire fantasies of a 'flowery mead' in the garden at home. For such treasures to hold their own in competition with the grass of an established lawn the fertility must be reduced. The vigour of turf can be lessened by close and frequent mowing for two or three years, removing the mowings so that they do not nourish the soil. If starting from scratch, the soil can be starved by raising crops of greedy vegetables like sweetcorn or courgettes.

Packets of wildflower seeds with such names as 'Farmer's Nightmare' are prepared specifically for different soil conditions but need careful supervision to make sure that invading thugs, such as rye grass, do not take over. The best way to raise almost all wild flowers, is to sow the seed in trays, grow the plants on, then transplant them into their positions with a bulb planter. This is particularly important if they are being inserted into established grass. Once this crop has flowered, it is essential not to mow until the flowers are over, the seed has set and dispersed.

Perhaps we should enjoy wild flowers in the country and concentrate on more predictable joys in the garden. A more controlled way of achieving colonies of native flowers is to make beds for them set off by shrubs and herbs, where they do not have to compete with grass. Columbines, daisies, sword lilies, violas, harebells and meadow crane's bills can be planted in drifts where colour and habit complement each other. Thus a medieval tapestry can be created by skill, design and cunning, rather than leaving it to chance.

The scent of June flowering shrubs, as lilac and wistaria give way to roses and mock orange, is perhaps the greatest incentive to stay at home. There are many beautiful shrub roses which are at the peak of their beauty in June but the best value are the hybrid musk roses. Only distantly connected with the musk rose from which they probably derive their vigour and old-fashioned perfume, they were bred by the Reverend J. Pemberton in the early part of this century. Requiring very little pruning and flowering twice, their flowers are borne in large trusses like a floribunda rose. 'Cornelia' has small formal buds of coppery apricot which open to a paler pink rosette. 'Felicia' has silvery pink flowers deepening in colour towards the centre with an aromatic fragrance. 'Penelope' blooms profusely with creamy pink flowers. 'Buff Beauty' is the odd one out, taking its colour from the yellow and buff end of the spectrum, so that it does not combine well with its cooler bluey-pink cousins but looks delightful contrasted with the pale lilac buddleia 'Lochinch'.

The first hint of mock orange, or *Philadelphus,* evokes memories of June evenings long past. 'Belle Etoile' with its semi-arching sprays of single white flowers, stained with a pinky-purple blotch, and 'Virginal' with enormous clusters of double pure white flowers, are the best large shrubs. The disadvantage of *Philadelphus* is the dullness of its foliage for the rest of the year but *Philadelphus coronarius* 'Aureus' has bright yellow foliage in the spring which glows in the shade, while *Philadelphus coronarius* 'Variegatus' has a creamy margin to its leaf which matches the creamy flowers. Their heavenly scent is indispensable to the magical sense of midsummer in the garden.

June

Reeds and water-lilies on Esthwaite Water

June

June

Photographs

July

A watercolour of Beatrix Potter's uncle's garden at
Gwaynynog, near Denbigh

The beginning of July is a golden moment in the garden when the feverish rush of growth peaks into flower. Now the gardener can stand still to survey his work and take a breathing space.

For English gardens, particularly, this is when what Russell Page, the great original English garden designer, called the "brightly coloured hay" of herbaceous planting comes into its prime. Many gardeners know that the classic herbaceous border is too extravagant of time and have artfully combined perennials with mixed plantings of shrubs and evergreen structural planting to create a series of seasonal effects. This month lady's mantle, pinks, campanulas, poppies, phlox, day lilies, golden rod and cornflowers make a glorious colourful impact.

Most evocative of midsummer is the scent of lavender, reminiscent of the seaside and the Mediterranean. It is justifiably popular as an aromatic border either side of the path from the gate to the front door. In July the shades and habits of different varieties can be appreciated: the most useful is *Lavandula* 'Hidcote', a deep indigo blue with grey evergreen foliage, it grows to about eighteen inches high and forms a thickset hedge. This makes a good edging to a gravel path or around evergreen shrubs, especially with white flowers. *Lavandula* 'Munstead' is a gentler blue, taller and looser, it makes an almost see-through higher hedge of hazy blue, which suits the pinks and pinky whites of old roses. A true Mediterranean lavender is *Lavandula stoechas* which is not really hardy but irresistible with its impudent pinky purple bracts. Lavenders only last about six years, when they begin to die off in bits. Hard trimming after

flowering can help to delay this deterioration but cuttings should be taken anyway, in case of frost casualties. Lavender sometimes selfseeds in gravel paths providing a constant supply of juvenile replacements for aging parents.

Long evenings in July, the warmest month of the year, are the time to complete leisurely maintenance tasks. Taking the wheelbarrow and secateurs, enjoy the evening scents from roses and cistus while cutting back early flowering plants such as delphiniums, lupins and purple flowering sage, which will flower again if cut back severely, just before flowering is over. Scabious, chamomile, sweet peas and yarrow all flower longer if they are cut as they fade, or to use in the house. Cut deadheads from paeonies with secateurs but leave the handsome foliage to die back naturally, using it to mask the wiry lower stems of lilies. Remove the faded blooms of roses and prune back to a new flowering bud to encourage autumn blooms. Look out for greenfly, blackspot, mildew or rust and spray promptly. Check climbing plants, tuck in this year's growth and tie in wall trained shrubs.

With so much to choose from in July it can be difficult to anticipate how enjoyable a cool combination of colours and freshness in this hot and sometimes humid month can be. A colony of tree poppies set off by a cool evergreen background, is a ravishing sight. With grey-green glaucous leaves, on stalks four or five feet high, the loose, open poppy flowers have petals like pleated white silk round a ball of deep golden stamens. The combination of Californian vigour and lovely delicate flowers is peculiarly satisfying.

A midsummer border can easily become too hot in colour but there are some cool blues, mauves and whites which reverse this trend. The bellflower, *Campanula lactiflora,* with lavender-blue bell-shaped flowers, though it grows up to five feet high, does not need staking. Chinese lilies flaunt beautiful white, trumpet-shaped flowers, streaked inside with yellow and outside with purple, arching back to show a pale yellow throat and yellow stamens, and emanate a luxurious scent, an indispensable ingredient of a July evening.

July

Side entrance to Melford Hall in Sussex

July

July

Corner of garden with flowerbeds and beehives

August

A cottage porch, 25 August 1909

August is the summer holiday month. The weather is often the same as July: a wet July will frequently be followed by a wet August, the kind of summer Britain is notorious for; or a hot July will be followed by a baking August with the garden gasping for water. The countryside begins to take on a bleached look, foliage seems heavier, grasses fade to hay, and cereal crops become golden cornfields ripe for harvest. Sunny days set the mood for packing up picnic baskets and setting off for favourite haunts beside pools, streams or lakes, spreading the table cloth in the shade and enjoying feeling close to the earth.

In the garden this golden theme can be picked up and developed into a glowing yellow colour scheme. Some flowering shrubs, such as cinquefoil with primrose yellow flowers, are at their best this month. St. John's wort, *Hypericum* 'Hidcote' is covered with saucer-shaped buttercup yellow flowers. The perennial yarrow, *Achillea* 'Moonshine', produces sulphur yellow flat flower heads on stout stems with finely cut grey foliage and associates well with evening primrose's clear yellow flowers. Height can be added by planting mullein with its velvety silver spikes topped with yellow flowers. As a contrast, African lilies begin flowering this month. Their bold, strap-like leaves are now crowned with globes of sparkling blue or white lily-like flowers.

Even the most workaholic gardeners can relax into a vacation mood this month. Rain will encourage the lawn to grow but there is plenty of time for grass cutting during the long evenings. If it is hot and dry, watering develops into a nightly ritual, carried out in the cool stillness of the evening.

Watering can become a chore and it is better to give beds a good soaking once a week than a sprinkling every day. A leisurely stroll round the garden will reveal many little tasks to be done, such as tying in rampant climbers and deadheading roses and herbaceous plants. It is worth considering whether seedheads may be more attractive than a cropped plant, as it is unlikely that plants flowering after July will flower again if cut back now.

This is the time when all sorts of 'holes' develop in herbaceous schemes, as plants go over. The maximum time for any classic herbaceous border to look its best is about six weeks. Traditionally, these gaps were filled by plants such as lilies grown in pots which were sunk into the ground to prolong the life of a flagging colour scheme. A less laborious ruse is to infill with annuals, such as tobacco plants, larkspur, love-in-the-mist, poppies, or sweet peas.

Architectural plants, which remain firm and unfading during a long hot summer are invaluable. Bear's breeches contributes its statuesque form, mauve and white hooded flowers and its superb glossy leaves. The globe artichoke works on a larger scale with jagged grey-green leaves. Thistle-like plants, such as the globe thistle and the teasel-like *Eryngium giganteum* 'Miss Wilmott's Ghost' with spiny, almost metallic, flowers are long lasting and eye-catching in August. Russian sage, *Perovskia* 'Blue Spire', becomes a cloud of tiny violet-blue flowers supported by fine silvery foliage in late summer.

Perhaps the most magical blossoming in August is that of *Magnolia grandiflora*. This evergreen shrub requires a sheltered south facing wall to thrive with its large leathery glossy leaves, whose undersides seem to be covered with rust covered felt. It is very distinguished and its flowers are no disappointment: creamy, ivory and waxy, they make large bowls of petals filled with a luscious lemon fragrance.

Another treat from an architectural plant in August is the beginning of the fruiting season for figs. To get good crops it is essential, when planting a fig tree, to restrict its roots. Dig a hole three feet square and three feet deep in the planting position and line the base and sides with bricks or concrete, leaving drainage holes. Fill the hole with good garden soil, into which have been mixed two pounds of bone meal.

August

An unused background study of garden beds for
The Tale of the Flopsy Bunnies

August

August

Photographs

September

Study of a wall with a climbing rose and pear tree

I don't believe grass will ever grow well under the fir tree, I was wondering whether white Japanese anemonies [sic] would grow where it is rather shaded, Millie says you have them in your garden & know their habits.

Letter to Mrs Fruing Warne, 26 September 1905

Midway between the height of summer and a shivery anticipation of winter, September is the watershed of the year. Warm sunny days and baked soil mean that any rain will extend the growing season and the garden has a mellow, maturing quality.

The gardener's task of checking ripening fruit can hardly be called a chore with its pleasures for eye, nose and tastebuds, as fresh, juicy plums, pears and then apples are sampled to assess whether the crop is ready to be picked. Victoria plums are followed by Williams and Conference pears, with Doyenne de Comice ripening in November. Amongst the numerous sequence of apples are Beauty of Bath, James Grieve, Ellison's Orange, Egremont Russet, Bramley Seedling and Tydeman's Late Orange.

You do not need an orchard to enjoy growing your own fruit. Espalier trees always look splendid in their traditional position trained against a south or west facing wall but they can be used as a high partition between different areas of the garden. In country gardens they are used as a screen around the vegetable garden or as a kind of rustic trellis. They bring a cottage garden quality, which cannot be matched by a ready-made trellis from the garden centre. The trained herringbone skeleton of horizontal branches comes to life in the spring with blossom, then leaves and fruit. The structure can be used as host to a series of climbers and decorative clematis. There is a delightful choice of late summer clematis: between the large flowered hybrids like violet *Jackmanii superba*; the pointed bright yellow lanterns of *Clematis tangutica*, whose attractive seedheads become silvery, silky tassels; and *Clematis viticella* with bell shaped nodding flowers of purple, mauve or white.

Blue and gold are the colours of an Indian summer. Late September sunshine illuminates all the variations on the theme of daisy-like blooms: marguerites, all sorts of chrysanthemums, from the self seeding feverfew and September flower with their classic simple white daisies and yellow centres to florists' pompoms; cornflowers; Michaelmas daisies with their jungle of single lavender blue daisies; cone flowers, black-eyed and slightly unkempt; and sneezeweed with its dark velvety knobby centres and turned-back petals. All these sunbursts of petals evoke images of cornfields and ripening crops - the countryside infiltrating the garden and reaching close to the house. The slight acidity in the odours of these late perennials is an unmistakeable hint that the year is moving on. The colour mood changes from cool, mauvey blues to the fiery tones of yellow and red, orange and bronze. In contrast with this extrovert display is the moonlight white and pink of Japanese anemones demurely lurking in the half shade.

Enjoy the lazy sunshine of a September afternoon, aware of a suggestion of a chill in the breeze. Inevitably, there are plenty of faded perennials which must be cut back and cleared, but there are some compensations. A new palette of enamel bright colours emerges now, particularly the bright blues of the various plumbagoes. *Ceratostigma willmottianum*, a shrub which waits until September to surprise you with speedwell-blue flowers on its twiggy branches, is covered with cobalt flowers. It loves a dry, sunny position where it attracts butterflies, especially Red Admiral and Painted Lady. The herbaceous carpeting plumbago, *Ceratostigma plumbagnoides*, makes a strong mat, running between early flowering shrubs and roses, keeping to a discreet foot high and displaying petite lapis lazuli blue flowers followed by red tinted leaves, which associate well with steely blue rue. In the greenhouse, a remote relation, *Plumbago capensis,* a true powder blue wall shrub, revives lingering memories of the Mediterranean, where it cascades down white washed walls.

September

A greenhouse in the gardens of Fawe Park, Derwentwater

September

September

Cold frame at Bedwell Lodge,
1891

October

This watercolour of *Clitocybe nebularis* is an example of
Beatrix Potter's beautifully observed fungus paintings

The countryside in October begins to change its mood dramatically from the faded straw colours of late summer. Cooler days stimulate purposeful activity: tractors are busy ploughing and cultivating a fine tilth ready for sowing. The texture of the fields becomes an immaculately raked, matt, rich, brown corduroy contrasting with cool grey dull skies.

The best pictures in October are not man made: pewter coloured skies are a foil to the glowing metallic colours of autumn leaves - brass, bronze and copper. Greeny gold translucent poplar leaves quiver and shimmer, backlit by the slanting rays of the low autumn sun. Along woodland verges bracken makes a waist-high swathe of russet, and fungi, which so fascinated Beatrix Potter, mount their annual fruit show of baroque and rococco shapes and frills. The colours of the leaf canopy evoke the warm tones of a cargo of spices - cinnamon, paprika, ginger, amber, sandalwood and tangerine.

Against the mellow harmonising tones of nature, gardens seem to make a gaudy show: crimson and green ribbons decorate the stag's horn sumach; Persian ironwood turns red, orange and gold; the spindle tree is decorated with vermilion fruit and bright pink foliage; the tulip tree's elegantly cut leaves turn barley-sugar golden and the maple-lobed leaves of sweet gum make a firework display of spectacular scarlet effects. But these distractions cannot avert the inevitable. Try as they might, soaring, swooping and sailing from the heights, leaves eventually plummet to earth and form a brittle, rustling carpet. Eventually, the brave show

show of paeony foliage, coppery pink and gleaming in the sunshine, is spoiled by rain and reduced to dark brown stalks.

October is a busy time, like the farmer clearing away last season's harvest and ploughing, the gardener must clear away and burn spent growth, and then dig beds over. Compost should be spread around shrubs to feed and protect their roots through the winter.

The autumn is an excellent time to review the garden and to record the successes and failures of the last year. Time now is well spent contemplating and analysing which combinations worked well and which did not; where gaps developed and which plants were disappointing and should be scrapped. There is plenty of scope for change and developing new planting plans, next summer already alive in the imagination. Looking at the whole garden and thinking about the overall balance of light and shade, mass and void, you might decide that now is the time to design a new bed, dig it over and leave the soil for the frost to get and break down over the winter, ready for planting in March.

Perennials can be moved now without sulking and new plants ordered from the nursery. New perennials and biennuals that have been raised from seed can be placed in their future flowering positions. Towards the end of the month new deciduous trees and shrubs can be planted.

When all this seems too much like hard work, there are all kinds of hidden delights to be discovered amongst damp grass and leaves or tucked away shyly, close to tree trunks camouflaged by snowberries. Some autumn bulbs are like old friends, returning year after year in increased numbers. The ivy leaved cyclamen is exquisite with its amethyst bright pink scented flowers pushing their way upwards before the leaves appear. The silver tracery on the leaves is said to be unique to each plant and therefore infinite in its variations. *Cyclamen hederifolium* seed themselves generously and young seedlings can be retrieved and nurtured in seed trays in the spring. Another plant of diminutive charms is lily turf, whose small pokers seem to be encrusted with pale mauve beads.

October

A walled garden at Lakefield (now Eeswyke), Sawrey

October

October

GARDEN DESIGN

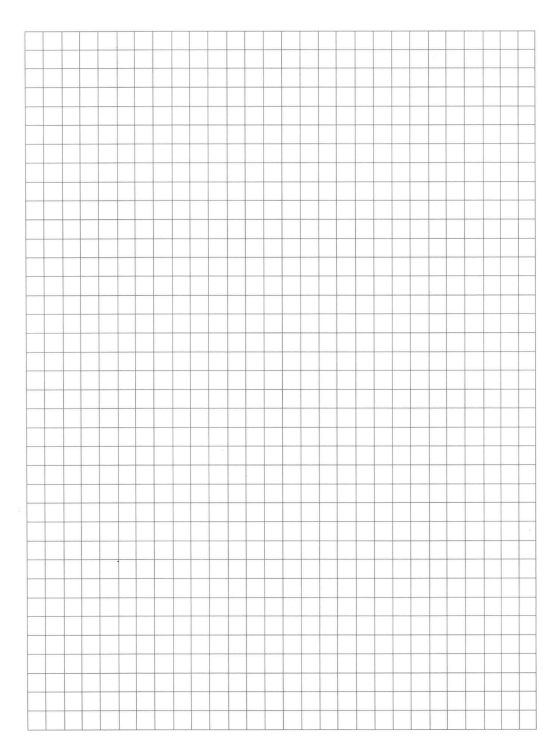

November

'Falling leaves' in the garden at Gwaynynog

The autumn frost spreads a ruddy glow over the land.
I shall never forget the view I once saw from Essendon Hill, miles
upon miles of golden oakwood with here and there a yellow streak of stubble
and a clump of russet walnut trees behind the red gable and the
thin blue smoke of a farm.

Memories of Camfield Place, Journal c. 1891

Trees and woodland are caught in a dramatic last blaze of colour in November, like a fire which flares up before dying down to a few embers. Beech leaves produce a burst of luminous orange, oak leaves turn the colour of ginger biscuits and birch leaves look like a shower of golden pennies before dropping.

The most obvious task of the autumn tidy up is dealing with fallen leaves. Traditionally, these went on the bonfire but now gardeners are more aware of replenishing the soil there is more interest in finding ways of taking a tip from nature and making leaf mould. If you have sufficient room to store sacks, collect as many garden leaves as you can, excluding beech and oak which are too tough, and put them in plastic sacks, which have been punctured to allow the action of tiny fungi.

Sprinkle the contents with compost activator for more rapid results, or with a little diluted liquid seaweed, if you can wait for a year, and store in a woodshed. You will be rewarded with a crumbly, dark mould to use as a mulch or to hoe into poor soil to improve its structure.

As the garden becomes more stark with the emergence of bare branches we can appreciate the rich decoration of hips and berries, shining in the clear autumn light. The berries of the common mountain ash are rapidly eaten by birds but some of the more unusual varieties seem bird resistant. *Sorbus hupehensis* has finely cut grey-green leaves, which become clear red in the autumn accompanied by loose clusters of pale green berries turning pinkish white, and *Sorbus* 'Joseph Rock' has orange brown leaves and berries which mature from pale primrose yellow to bright amber. Crab apple trees come in many varieties with different virtues but *Malus* 'Red Sentinel' produces the biggest and best berries in clusters of sealing wax red apples which persist through the winter. *Malus* 'John Downie' has conical fruits which are orange scarlet and make delectable crab apple jelly, fresh and sharp. Glowing yellow fruit adorn *Malus* 'Golden Hornet' until midwinter.

Shrubs, like viburnums, cotoneaster and firethorn, contribute to the immense range of berry colours and tones, ranging through blues, oranges, reds and yellows. The native guelder rose provides translucent red clusters, while bright turquoise blue berries appear on female plants of *Viburnum davidii*. Cotoneasters are the most spectacular, especially *Cotoneaster henryanus* with elegant long sprays of crimson berries set off by dark green pointed leathery leaves.

The weather in November begins to get the better of most gardeners. Plants stop growing when the temperature falls below 43 degrees Fahrenheit. This is the best time to plant bare rooted, dormant trees and shrubs such as roses, as the root system can work actively in the ground, still relatively warm from the summer, until it gets too cold. Plants will be given a good start if the area round the base of the plant is kept free of competition by means of a mulch.

This is the worst month of the year for cutting flowers, although the prudent flower arranger may have gathered dried hydrangeas and grasses with ornamental seedheads. Some roses, however, persevere. The China roses: 'Cecile Brunner' or sweetheart rose; and 'Perle d'Or', with their subtly different tones of blue-pink and apricot, are still producing delicate buds on twiggy bushes. Another half China, polyantha rose, 'Nathalie Nypels' greets you cheerfully with bunches of small rosy-pink, rambler like flowers on compact bushes until December.

November

Hawthorn and snowberry

November

November

Farmhouse at Brookthorpe

December

A study of squirrels and mistletoe

There has been time for reading lately; outside work is
mostly finished for the season, and the country is rainswept
and misty - but always beautiful.

Letter to Helen Dean Fish, an American editor of
children's books, 8 December 1934

December can be a dark, desolate month when garden work is difficult
because of gales and rain. On clear days, however, many views which
are obscured by leaves during the summer are revealed. Winter
austerity strips trees back to their skeletons and the garden back to the
bare bones of its structure.

In the winter, the patterns made by the shape of lawns, paths, hedges,
pergolas, trellis, or trained trees become distinct. Suddenly structures,
like wrought iron gates or fences, become important as their shadows are
emphasised and elongated by the low winter sunshine. It is also the time
when evergreen plants come into their own, either as reinforcing the
pattern of the design of the garden, or as freestanding sculptures in their
own right. These sculptures might be clipped and shaped as topiary, or
free forms like junipers or yuccas which make a dramatic impact.

Evergreen shrubs can be used as architecture in the garden: making
walls, which provide a vital backdrop to more delicate, insubstantial
plants which would be lost without a setting; providing buttresses and
bookends to collections of precious plants which might become shapeless
and untidy without a retaining structure. Box hedges are particularly
effective for this purpose and are used in Spanish gardens to make a
frame round ephemeral flowering plants like pale paeonies and white
roses. In Britain box has been used for centuries to make knot gardens,
which are magically enhanced in
winter by frost or snow which
outlines the solid green pattern.
Box globes are transformed into
huge white snowballs.

As well as shape, evergreen plants provide
colour and texture in the winter. Velvety

lamb's ears beautifully complement the tiny glaucous leaves on wiry stems of *Hebe* 'Quicksilver', variations on silver beside a path. Steely blue rue contrasts with the maroon seedheads of sedum and harmonizes with the evergreen foliage of pinks, spurge and *Convolvulus cneorum*. Golden foliage lights up in the winter sunshine, especially the golden marked ivies like *Hedera helix* 'Buttercup' and 'Goldheart', and Persian ivy, *Hedera colchica* 'Dentata Variegata'. There is a great range of different hollies, silver-edged and gold-edged, mottled and variegated, whose berry colour differs as much as the foliage. Perhaps the most handsome of evergreen shrubs is *Mahonia japonica*, whose pinnate glossy leaves, like bergenia leaves, are tipped with crimson as the frost touches them. Some of the lemon-yellow mahonia flowers with their lily-of-the-valley scent will be out by Christmas.

Midwinter is the time to take hardwood cuttings, one of the easiest and most satisfying ways of propagating woody plants, like willows, dogwoods, escallonia, flowering currants, tamarisk, the smoke tree and garrya. Stem cuttings are taken from fully ripe wood at the end of the growing season. The usual method is to cut a selection of pencil-thick twigs, trimmed to a length of ten to twelve inches. Remove the lower leaves and cut the stems straight across at right angles at a leaf node. Sappy growth at the tip should be removed with a slanting cut, which will shed the rain and also tell you which way up your cuttings are. Hardwood cuttings are inserted in the open, to make roots before being planted out the following year. First, make a V-shaped trench, about a spade's depth, one side of which should be vertical to support the cuttings. Sprinkle coarse sand at the bottom to encourage rooting and drainage. When the cuttings are in place, the furrow should be half filled with soil, firmed and then topped up.

There are a few invaluable winter-flowering plants which delight our hearts during these cold dark days. If only one tree could be chosen for a small garden, on the short list must be the winter-flowering cherry. Since November it has been in blossom. Even though the frost catches it repeatedly, it produces crop after crop of fresh pinkish-white flowers. The shoots can be cut and brought inside to flower.

December

Snow scene of Sawrey, painted from
Tower Bank Arms

December

LATIN NAMES

Aconite	*Aconitum* spp.	Ox-eye	*Leucanthemum vulgare*
Anemone, Wood	*Anemone nemerosa*	Michaelmas	*Aster* spp.
Artichoke, Globe	*Cynara Scolymus*		
Azalea	*Azalea* spp.	Delphinium	*Delphinium* spp.
		Dogwood	*Cornus* spp.
Bay tree	*Laurus nobilis*		
Bellflower	*Campanula persicifolia*	Feverfew	*Chrysanthemum*
Birch, Silver	*Betula pendula*		*parthenium*
Blackthorn	*Prunus spinosa*	Fig tree	*Ficus carica*
Bleeding heart, White	*Dicentra spectabilis 'Alba'*	Foam flower	*Tiarella cordifolia*
Bluebell	*Endymion* spp.	Foxglove	*Digitalis* spp.
Box	*Buxus* spp.		
Bugle	*Ajuga reptans*	Glory-of-the-snow	*Chionodoxa luciliae*
Buttercup	*Ranunculus* spp.	Golden rod	*Solidago* spp.
		Guelder rose	*Viburnum* spp.
Campion, Red	*Silene diocia*		
Chamomile	*Anthemis* spp.	Harebell	*Campanula rotundifolia*
Chrysanthemum	*Chrysanthemum* spp.	Hazel	*Corylus avellana*
Cinquefoil, Shrubby	*Potentilla fruticosa*	Hellebore, Stinking	*Helleborus foetidus*
Clematis	*Clematis* spp.	Holly	*Ilex* spp.
Clover, Red	*Trifolium pratense*	Honesty	*Lunaria biennis*
White	*Trifolium repens*	Honeysuckle, Winter	*Lonicera fragrantissima*
Columbine	*Aquilegia* spp.	Hosta	*Hosta* spp.
Cone flower	*Rudbeckia hirta*	Hydrangea	*Hydrangea* spp.
Corncockle	*Agrostemma githago*		
Cornflower	*Centaurea* spp.	Ivy, Persian	*Hedera colchica 'Dentata Variegata'*
Cotoneaster	*Cotoneaster* spp.		
Cowslip	*Primula veris*		
Crab Apple, Wild	*Malus sylvestris*	Jasmine, Winter-flowering	*Jasminum nudiflorum*
Cranesbill	*Geranium* spp.	Juniper	*Juniperus*
Crocus	*Crocus* spp.		
Currant, Flowering	*Ribes sanguineum*	Lady's mantle	*Alchemilla mollis*
		Lamb's ear	*Stachys lanata*
Daffodil	*Narcissus* spp.	Larkspur	*Delphinium ajacis*
Daisy, Common	*Bellis perennis*	Lavender	*Lavandula* spp

LATIN NAMES

Lilac	*Syringa* spp.	Snowdrop	*Galanthus* spp.
Lily, African	*Agapanthus africanus*	Snowy mespilus	*Amelanchier canadensis*
Day	*Hemerocallis* spp.	Solomon's seal	*Polygonatum multiflorum*
Chinese	*Lilium regale*	Spanish squill	*Scilla hispanica*
Lily-of-the-valley	*Convallaria majalis*	Spindle tree	*Euonymus europaeus*
Lily Turf	*Liriope muscari*	Spurge	*Euphorbia* spp.
Lords-and-ladies, Italian	*Arum Italicum* 'Pictum'	Staghorn sumach	*Rhus typhina*
Lungwort	*Pulmonaria*	Sweet gum	*Liquidambar*
		Sweet pea	*Lathyrus odoratus*
Magnolia	*Magnolia* spp.		
Mahonia	*Mahonia* spp	Thistle, Globe	*Echinops ritro*
Mexican orange blossom	*Choisya ternata*	Tobacco plant	*Nicotiana sylvestris*
Mock orange	*Philadelphus* spp.	Tree paeony	*Paeony suffruticosa*
Mountain ash	*Sorbus aucuparia*	Tree poppy	*Romneya coulteri*
Mullein	*Verbascum*	Tulip tree	*Liriodendron tulipifera*
Orpine	*Sedum telephium*	Viburnum	*Viburnum* spp.
		Violet, Dog's tooth	*Erythronium dens-canis*
Paeony	*Paeonia* spp.		
Pear tree	*Pyrus* spp.	Whitebeam	*Sorbus aria*
Persian ironwood	*Parrotica persica*	Willow, Goat	*Salix caprea*
Phlox	*Phlox* spp.	Black	*Salix nigricans*
Pink	*Dianthus* spp.	Windflower	*Anemone blanda*
Plum, Orchard	*Prunus domestica*	Winter sweet	*Chimonanthus praecox*
Poppy, Common	*Papaver rhoeas*	Wistaria	*Wistaria* spp.
Primrose	*Primula vulgaris*	Witch Hazel	*Hamamelis mollis*
Rhododendron	*Rhododendron* spp.	Yarrow	*Achillea millefolium*
Rose, Christmas	*Helleborus niger*	Yew	*Taxus baccata*
Lenten	*Helleborus orientalis*		
Sage, Purple flowering	*Salvia superba*		
St. John's wort	*Hypericum* 'Hidcote'		
Scabious	*Scabiosa* spp.		
Sneezeweed	*Helenium* spp.		

GARDEN DESIGN

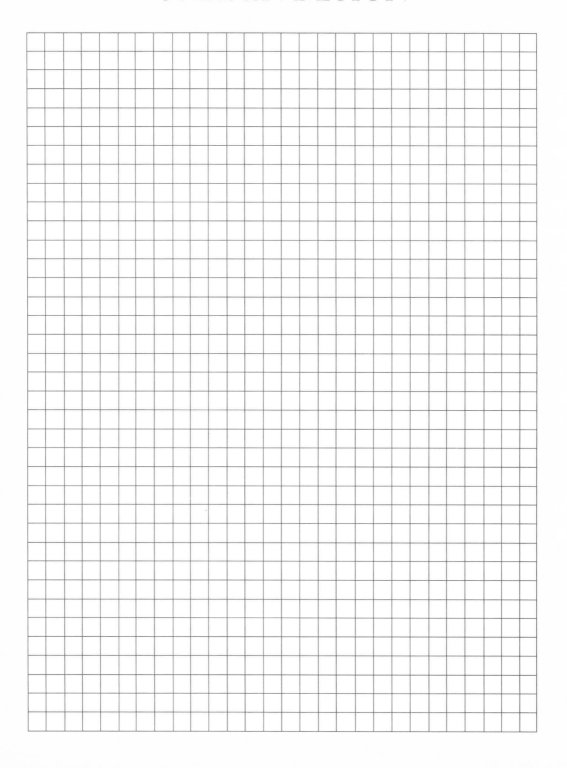

GARDEN DESIGN

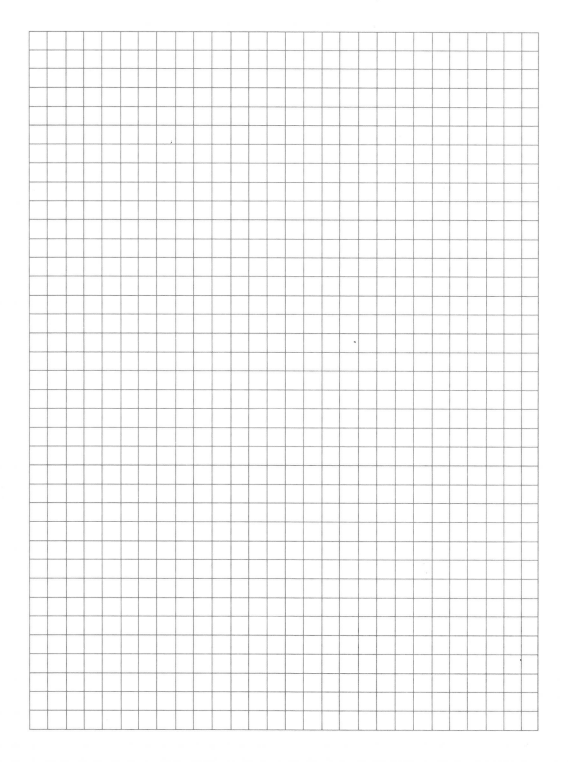

New Plants to Grow

PLANT	CONDITIONS REQUIRED

New Plants to Grow

COLOUR, HEIGHT AND FLOWERING TIME

Seeds and Bulbs Ordered

ITEM	ORDERED & RECEIVED

Seeds and Bulbs Ordered

SUPPLIER	QUANTITY & COST

Propagation Record

PLANT

Propagation Record

DATE STARTED	DATE ROOTED OR GERMINATED	DATE MOVED OUTDOORS

Addresses

NAME

ADDRESS

TELEPHONE

NAME

ADDRESS

TELEPHONE

NAME

ADDRESS

TELEPHONE

NAME

ADDRESS

TELEPHONE

NAME

ADDRESS

TELEPHONE

NAME

ADDRESS

TELEPHONE

NAME

ADDRESS

TELEPHONE

NAME

ADDRESS

TELEPHONE

NAME

ADDRESS

TELEPHONE

NAME

ADDRESS

TELEPHONE

NAME

ADDRESS

TELEPHONE

NAME

ADDRESS

TELEPHONE

A view along a buttressed wall at
Melford Hall in Suffolk

Addresses

NAME

ADDRESS

TELEPHONE

NAME

ADDRESS

TELEPHONE

NAME

ADDRESS

TELEPHONE

NAME

ADDRESS

TELEPHONE

NAME

ADDRESS

TELEPHONE

NAME

ADDRESS

TELEPHONE

NAME

ADDRESS

TELEPHONE

NAME

ADDRESS

TELEPHONE

NAME

ADDRESS

TELEPHONE

NAME

ADDRESS

TELEPHONE

NAME

ADDRESS

TELEPHONE

NAME

ADDRESS

TELEPHONE

Addresses

NAME

ADDRESS

TELEPHONE

NAME

ADDRESS

TELEPHONE

NAME

ADDRESS

TELEPHONE

NAME

ADDRESS

TELEPHONE

NAME

ADDRESS

TELEPHONE

NAME

ADDRESS

TELEPHONE

NAME

ADDRESS

TELEPHONE

NAME

ADDRESS

TELEPHONE

NAME

ADDRESS

TELEPHONE

NAME

ADDRESS

TELEPHONE

NAME

ADDRESS

TELEPHONE

NAME

ADDRESS

TELEPHONE

The gardening notes that appear for each month in this book
are based on a moderate climate. Planting and flowering
times will vary if you live in a very
warm or very cool area.